TRUNDLEBERRY MANOR

MR BOUNCER'S
HOUSE

FIRE
STATION

BLODGER'S
GATEHOUSE

SIGMUND SWAMP'S
HOUSE & BOATHOUSE

FERNYBANK FERRY

BROCK GRUFFY'S
SHOP

BRAMBLE'S FARM

CHURCH

VICARAGE

RAILWAY STATION

P.C. HOPPIT'S
HOUSE

POLICE
STATION

DR. BUSHY'S
HOUSE

N

This book belongs to:

SPORTS DAY

Written & Illustrated by John Patience

PUBLISHED BY PETER HADDOCK LIMITED, BRIDLINGTON, ENGLAND.
© FERN HOLLOW PRODUCTIONS LIMITED
PRINTED IN ITALY
ISBN 0 7105 0123 4

It was still very early in the morning, but some of the Fern Hollow animals were already busily preparing for the Sports Day, which, as usual, was to be held in one of Farmer Bramble's fields. Spike and Patch had been given the job of painting the white lines for the running lanes.

Meanwhile,
on the edge of the
field, Mr. Chips whistled happily
to himself as he went about the business of
putting up a refreshments stand.
"It's beginning to look quite splendid, Mr. Chips."
exclaimed Mr. Acorn, who was supplying the cakes and
buns.
"It certainly is," agreed Mr. Crackleberry, rolling a big
barrel of orange juice off the back of his wagon.
"I hope the weather stays fine though—there's a big
black cloud over there on the horizon."

At Trundleberry Manor, Lord Trundle packed the sports day prizes into a trunk and carried them out to his car. He too noticed the dark cloud on the horizon, but he was in too much of a hurry to give it much thought and, jumping into the car, he drove off to the sports field.

Suddenly, as he was driving over the bridge by the Jolly Vole Hotel, Lord Trundle's car hit a big stone lying in the road.

It was such a hard bump
that the trunk containing
the prizes shot off the roof
rack and with a great
SPLOSH!
landed in the River Ferny.

Luckily the trunk floated, but it was soon caught in the current and swept away down the river. "Oh no!" panted Lord Trundle, rushing along the river bank. "What ever shall we do?"

The Sports Day prizes would certainly have been lost if it had not been for Sigmund Swamp, who was out fishing, and seeing the trunk floating by, cast out his line and caught it, just as if it had been a great big fish!

It turned out that Sigmund had quite forgotten that it was the Sports Day, and was very pleased when Lord Trundle offered him a lift in his car. By the time they arrived at the sports field, the tug of war was about to begin, but the big black cloud was now directly overhead.

Each of the two teams led by P.C. Hoppit and Brock Gruffy got a firm grip on the rope. Boris Blink slowly raised the starting pistol and — BANG — the contest began.

A few moments later the big black cloud burst.
The rain came pouring down and, in next to no
time, the field became waterlogged.
The tug of war teams slipped and slid around
in the mud, fell into the puddles and looked
quite ridiculous.

Everyone ran for the shelter of the trees or the refreshments stand, where they all stood around looking very glum. It looked as if the Sports Day would have to be cancelled. The sky was now completely covered with clouds and the rain was falling harder all the time!

Then Lord Trundle had a wonderful idea.
"Everyone is invited to Trundleberry Manor," he cried.
"We'll hold the Sports Day indoors!"
All the animals agreed that it was a fine idea and they
quickly made their way to the Manor.

The sack race was held in
the great hall, and was won by
Dipper Croaker, who, being
a frog, could hop further
and faster than anyone,
even in a sack!

The egg and spoon race up and down the
main staircase was great fun. Clarence
Hoppit was in the lead for most of the
way, but he dropped his egg and
Dusty Rusty won by a whisker.

Then came the special event, the bannister slide. The contestants slid down the bannister, flew off the end, and landed on a mattress. Spike Willowbank won this quite easily, but he overshot the mattress and landed on top of Brock Gruffy!

When the games were all over, Sigmund Swamp set up
his camera to take a picture of the prize giving ceremony.
"Smile everyone." said Sigmund.

Everyone did smile and it made a marvellous picture!

Fern Hollow

MR. CHIPS'S HOUSE

MR. WILLOWBANK'S COBBLER'S SHOP

MR. CROAKER'S WATERMILL

STRIPEY'S HOUSE

SCHOOL

THE JOLLY VOLE HOTEL

RIVER FERNY

MR ACORN'S BAKERY

MR. RUSTY'S HOUSE

MR. PRICKLES'S HOUSE

POST OFFICE

BORIS BLINKS'S BOOKSHOP

MR. TWINKLE'S HOUSE

MR. TUTTLEBEE'S SHOP

MR. THIMBLE'S TAILORS SHOP

WINDYWOOD